PERFECT PIGS

❧ An Introduction to Manners ❧

Marc Brown and Stephen Krensky

JOY STREET BOOKS

Little, Brown and Company

Boston   Toronto   London

For the sow sisters
Colleen and Kim

HC: 10 9 8 7 6

PB: 10 9 8

Library of Congress Cataloging in Publication Data

Brown, Marc Tolon.
  Perfect pigs.

  Summary: A simple introduction to good manners to use with family, friends, at school, during meals, with pets, on the phone, during games, at parties, and in public places.
  1. Etiquette for children and youth. [1. Etiquette]
I. Krensky, Stephen. II. Title.
BJ1857.C5B67 1983   395′.122   83-746
ISBN 0-316-11079-5
ISBN 0-316-11080-9 (pbk.)

JOY STREET BOOKS
ARE PUBLISHED BY
LITTLE, BROWN AND COMPANY (INC.)

AHS

*Published simultaneously in Canada
by Little, Brown & Company (Canada) Limited*

PRINTED IN THE UNITED STATES OF AMERICA

Contents

At All Times

Take care of the property of others, as well as your own.

Remember that you can't always get your own way.

I KNEW THESE ALREADY. DOESN'T EVERYONE?

5

Around the House

Wipe your feet before coming inside.

Knock on the door before entering a room.

Play quietly if someone is sleeping.

NEATNESS AND CONSIDERATION ARE MY TRADEMARKS.

7

With Your Family

Ask to borrow things, and return them when you're done.

Let others know you care about them.

Use words to solve arguments instead of fighting.

IN MY FAMILY, EVERYONE PULLS HIS OWN WEIGHT.

8

Help out with chores.

On the Telephone

When making a call, give your name, then ask for the person you wish to speak to.

When answering a call . . .

Don't call friends too early in the morning . . .
or too late at night.

When someone can't come to the phone . . .

MAY I TAKE A MESSAGE?

OF COURSE I HAVE PIGS' FEET. WHAT DO YOU MEAN, IF I WEAR SHOES NO ONE WILL NOTICE?

During Meals

Wash your hands before eating.

Ask politely for food that you can't reach.

When you sit down, put your napkin on your lap.
Use it to wipe your hands and mouth.

13

Use the right utensil or dish.

14

Be willing to try new foods.

Ask to be excused before leaving the table.

With Pets

Train your pet to be friendly, but not too friendly.

Teach pets to play only with their own toys.

Don't feed pets during family meals.

Walk your pet on a leash.

Remember that a pet has feelings, too.

AND DON'T FORGET, A CLEAN PET IS A HAPPY PET.

Giving a Party

Send out your invitations at least a week ahead.

Introduce your guests to one another.

I'M VERY GOOD AT DOING DECORATIONS.

Offer refreshments to others before eating them yourself.

Spend some time with every guest.

When receiving presents, remember it's the thought that counts.

Going to a Party

Let the hosts know that you're coming so they can plan to include you.

Shake hands when meeting someone.

When choosing gifts,
think of what others would like,
not of what you would want.

Offer to help clean up.

Thank your host for inviting you.

WHAT DO YOU MEAN I WASN'T INVITED?

21

With Friends

Don't keep them waiting.

Share your toys.

I HAD A FRIEND ONCE... NO, MAYBE TWICE.

Don't make fun of others.

KICK ME

KICK ME HARD

22

Help friends when they need you.

Be a good listener, and share your own ideas, too.

At School

Pay attention to your teacher.

Wait your turn to speak.

During Games

Always obey the rules.

2-4-6-8 WHO DO WE OBLITERATE?

Don't lose your temper.

26

Be a good sport.

In Public Places

Give your seat to someone who needs it more than you do.

Wait patiently in lines.

Don't talk loudly or disturb others.

Hold a door open for anybody behind you.

Put litter in trash containers.

SOME PEOPLE HAVE NO CONSIDERATION FOR OTHERS!

29